RUBY MAE
Has Something to Say

DAVID SMALL

CROWN PUBLISHERS, INC. • *New York*

To my dear Miss McGillicuddy,
for endless help and kindness

Published by Crown Publishers, Inc., a Random House company, 225 Park Avenue South,
New York, New York 10003

CROWN is a trademark of Crown Publishers, Inc.
Manufactured in the United States of America

Library of Congress Cataloging-in-Publication Data

Small, David, 1945–
Ruby Mae has something to say / David Small.
p.   cm.
Summary: Tongue-tied Ruby Mae Foote fulfills her dream of speaking for world peace at the
United Nations when her nephew Billy Bob invents a device to solve her speech problem.
[1. Speech disorders—Fiction.   2. Inventions—Fiction.   3. United Nations—Fiction]   I. Title.
PZ7.S638Ru   1992
[E]—dc20   91-33785

ISBN 0-517-58248-1 (trade)
0-517-58249-X (lib. bdg.)
10 9 8 7 6 5 4 3 2 1   First Edition

The town of Nada, Texas, was small. You could stand on one side of town, whisper something, and be heard on the other side. It was *that* small.

Still, Nada had a few things in it. There was a general store, an abandoned train depot, a three-legged dog, and the World Headquarters for Universal Peace and Understanding.

The World Headquarters was in the home of Miss
Ruby Mae Foote.

Ruby Mae had a big dream: she wanted to speak at the
United Nations in New York City to deliver her message of
universal peace and understanding.

But Ruby Mae also had a big problem…

She was tongue-tied.
Sometimes she mixed up the letters of words.

Without meaning to, she insulted people.

At other times, for no apparent reason, she was just plain incomprehensible.

Because of this, the residents of Nada had written off Ruby Mae Foote as a goofball.

Billy Bob was Ruby Mae's young nephew. He wanted to be an inventor of things that would benefit all humanity. But try as he might, he could think of nothing new.

Then one day he had an idea. He went into the kitchen. Cupboard doors banged, drawers slammed, utensils clashed. Shortly Billy Bob emerged with his new invention.

It was an old colander with things wired on. Around the rim: a nutcracker, a bottle opener, and a pastry brush. On top: some holiday pine cones.

"Aunt Ruby Mae," he exclaimed, "your troubles are over! Put this on and get ready to give your message to the world!"

"Feel anything?" asked Billy Bob. Ruby Mae shook her head. The pine cones rattled dryly.

"Speak!" urged her nephew. He made a few adjustments. "Anything now?"

"Nothing, Bobby Bill," she replied. "I mean, Bolly Bib. I mean, Bibby Blob. I mean…"

Removing it from his aunt's head, the boy disappeared into the kitchen. Moments later he returned with a new, improved apparatus. He had taken off the pine cones and added a melon-ball scoop, a wire whisk, and a corkscrew standing upright.

And it worked!

Nothing daunted Ruby Mae now that she could talk straight. First she became mayor of Nada, then governor of Texas. Hers was a meteoric rise!

Curiously, she never appeared in public without a big hat on her head.

Billy Bob's invention was in need of a name. They called it the Bobatron.

As time went on, Billy Bob made additions and improvements to his original design. And as the Bobatron grew...

so grew Ruby Mae's hats.

At last it happened: Ruby Mae was invited to speak to the United Nations General Assembly in New York! Ruby Mae and Billy Bob took a taxi from the airport to the United Nations Plaza. For the special occasion she wore an enormous hat covered with doves of peace.

Then disaster struck.

With a rush of wings and a savage shriek, a pigeon hawk swooped down from a nearby skyscraper and snatched the hat in its powerful talons. Away the bird flew to some distant aerie, taking with it the doves of peace, the hat, *and the Bobatron!*

Ruby Mae looked pale and unnerved.

Billy Bob whispered, "Aunt Ruby Mae, I've been meaning to tell you, you don't *need* that old piece of junk on your head to speak well. It's all in your *mind.* You can give your message without it!"

Smiling weakly, Ruby Mae went into the auditorium.

Flashbulbs popped. Cameras whirred. Satellites shot pictures of Ruby Mae around the globe as she ascended to the podium. Guests from every nation in the world held their breath in eager anticipation of the words about to be spoken.

Ruby Mae cleared her throat, opened her mouth, and started to speak.

Her words were a meaningless babble.

In the translators' booth panic broke out. They pawed through the dictionaries of ninety-three languages but could not decipher one word. In the auditorium people tapped their earphones and shook their heads. Meanwhile, a small boy raced for the exit.

Billy Bob fled to the stairs and sped to the basement.

In the gigantic United Nations kitchen, hors d'oeuvres for six thousand were being prepared. Billy Bob had no time to explain. He ripped the necessary equipment from the hands of the chefs…

assembled it as the elevator rose back to the third floor...

ran to the podium, and clapped the Bobatron onto his
aunt's head.

As Ruby Mae turned to the audience, her head crowned with its tangle of copper, aluminum, tin, and wire, a mild titter arose in the room. The titter grew to a chorus of guffaws and cackles. At last the whole lot of world leaders was convulsed with laughter.

Then Ruby Mae Foote stepped forward and raised her hand for silence.

"My friends," she said in a level tone. "Leaders of the world, my message to you is simple: to achieve universal peace and understanding on this planet you have only to speak plainly, even though you may look foolish. This is a thousand times better than looking good and talking nonsense."

The planet Earth was small. You could stand on one side, whisper something, and be heard on the other side. It was *that* small.

Still, Earth had a few things on it. For one thing, it had Nada, Texas, Ruby Mae Foote, and the World Headquarters for Universal Peace and Understanding.